WHO BOB WHAT PANTS?

P9-DFK-327

adapted by Emily Sollinger
based on the screenplay by Casey Alexander,
Zeus Cervas, and Steven Banks
illustrated by Stephen Reed

SIMON SPOTLIGHT/NICKELODEON
New York   London   Toronto   Sydney

Stephen Hillenburg

Based on the TV series *SpongeBob SquarePants*® created by Stephen Hillenburg as seen on Nickelodeon®

SIMON SPOTLIGHT

An imprint of Simon & Schuster Children's Publishing Division

1230 Avenue of the Americas, New York, New York 10020

Manufactured in the United States of America

10 9

ISBN-13: 978-1-4169-6736-1

ISBN-10: 1-4169-6736-2

1009 LAK

"Good morning, Gary!" sang SpongeBob. "Isn't life great?" he asked, picking up Gary and hugging him a *little* too tightly. Gary let out a loud growl.

Later, on his way out, SpongeBob bumped right into his best friend, Patrick!

"Oh, hey, Patrick! How goes it?" SpongeBob asked.

"Great, until you showed up," muttered Patrick. "That *was* a cake for my mom's birthday," he continued, pointing to his chocolate-covered belly. "Thanks a lot. Now please just go away!"

SpongeBob frowned and walked away. Next he visited his good friend Squidward. But Squidward just slammed the door in SpongeBob's face! SpongeBob felt even worse than he had before.

SLAM!

He knew Sandy would be happy to see him. But as he walked into her treedome, he tripped and splashed the water from his helmet all over her brand-new robot. Sandy's face turned red with anger.

"Just GO!" she snarled.

There was only one hope left—the Krusty Krab! But as he entered the kitchen, SpongeBob slipped, slid across the floor, and knocked Mr. Krabs and his crisp dollar bills right into the fryer!

"If I were you, lad, I'd get as far away from me as possible!" Mr. Krabs barked.

Miserable, SpongeBob decided it was time to leave Bikini Bottom forever. "Good-bye, Bikini Bottom," SpongeBob called out. "Good-bye, life as I know it . . ."

After miles of walking, SpongeBob found himself in an unfamiliar place.
There were new sounds and scary creatures. It was dark, and suddenly
SpongeBob heard a loud noise! Afraid, he ran away as fast as he could.
As he ran, SpongeBob tripped on a rock and tumbled down a tall cliff,
bumping his head hard on the way down!

Meanwhile, back in Bikini Bottom, Patrick was knocking on SpongeBob's door when Sandy appeared.

"Patrick, where's SpongeBob?" she asked.

"I don't know. I've been knocking on his door for three hours."

Worried, she gave the door a quick karate chop. *Boom!* The door came crashing down. Inside, an oversized Gary let out a "meow."

"Oh, boy!" cried Sandy. "Gary said SpongeBob left a note."

Burp!

GARY

"He's gone! I shouldn't have yelled at SpongeBob," Sandy lamented. "I must have made him feel really bad."

"Me too," said Patrick.

"We have to find him!" said Sandy. "Come on! Let's start searchin'!"

Sandy and Patrick checked the Krusty Krab. SpongeBob wasn't there, but there *were* a lot of hungry customers who wanted their Krabby Patties. Mr. Krabs was really worried! He knew that the Krusty Krab couldn't survive without SpongeBob!

"I'm nothing without my number-one fry cook!" said Mr. Krabs. "Squidward, I am ordering you to find him. If you don't, you'll be out of a job forever! If you do find him, this jewel-encrusted egg will be yours to keep!"

"A jewel-encrusted egg?" asked Squidward, looking longingly at the egg. "My collection will finally be complete! I am on my way, sir."

Back in the unfamiliar seas, SpongeBob finally opened his eyes and rubbed the large bump on his head. Then he noticed two fish kneeling down, looking at a pile of square pants. He went over to say hello.

"Oh, hello! We were just admiring your clothes!" the fish told him. "These are your brown pants, aren't they?" the fish asked, showing him a pile of brown pants.

"I can't remember. I don't even know my name," said SpongeBob. "All I know is that I hit my head and woke up here."

"That's too bad. Let's call you Cheesehead BrownPants."

Just then SpongeBob felt something in his pockets. "Hey, what's this?" he said, pulling out a bottle of bubbles and a blowing wand.

"Not bubbles!" shouted his new friends. Then they ran away!

SpongeBob started walking. Soon he found himself in New Kelp City.

Grrr! His stomach began to growl loudly. He needed food, but he didn't have a penny in his pockets! There was only one thing to do—get a job.

But his fantastic bubble-blowing skills made every employer run away in fear.

I don't understand, thought SpongeBob. Is something wrong with this place, or is it me?

SpongeBob began walking around
the city aimlessly. To cheer himself
up, he took out his trusty bubbles
and began to blow. "Bubbles will
steady the old nerves," he said
to himself. *Bloop!* "Feeling better
already!"

Then, out of the dark shadows, came a group of scary-looking fish. They were big, they were mean, and they didn't want any bubbles on their turf! They called themselves the Bubble Poppin' Boys. They tried to catch SpongeBob, so he ran away as fast as he could.

POP!

Then SpongeBob had an idea! He blew the biggest bubble ever—and caught the Bubble Poppin' Boys inside! It floated far, far away with them inside, never to return.

Citizens of New Kelp City flooded the streets with bubbles in celebration!
"Thank you, Cheesehead BrownPants!" the mayor said to SpongeBob. "You
have restored bubble blowing to the streets! I appoint you the new mayor!"

Meanwhile . . . Sandy, Squidward, and Patrick continued their search.
"There he is!" exclaimed Sandy. "On the cover of that newspaper! He's
mayor of New Kelp City? We've got to get there, quick!"

When Sandy, Patrick, and Squidward got there, they were shocked by what they saw—and heard.

"Citizens of New Kelp City," announced SpongeBob over a microphone. "I'm not exactly sure what a 'mayor' is. But, as long as I am wearing this hat, it will always be safe to blow bubbles in New Kelp City, or my name isn't . . . CheeseHead BrownPants."

"CheeseHead BrownPants?" said Sandy.

"Who are you?" asked SpongeBob.

"We're your best friends!" said Patrick.

"Sorry. All I remember is hitting my head, blowing some bubbles, and now, poof! I'm mayor!"

"You must have lost your memory when you hit your head," said Sandy. "Come back to Bikini Bottom with us. We're all real sorry we yelled at you, buddy."

"I'm sorry," replied SpongeBob. "I can't leave. I'm late for a very important meeting." With that SpongeBob hopped in the mayor's limousine, which was waiting for him.

Good thing Squidward was in the driver's seat! "Don't just stand there," he called to Sandy and Patrick. "Get in!"

And off they rode, back to Bikini Bottom.

"Start fryin' up them Patties!" yelled Mr. Krabs cheerfully when he saw SpongeBob come through the door.

"I was a fry cook before?" asked SpongeBob, unimpressed.

"Yes, lad! The best in the business!" replied Mr. Krabs proudly.

"Well, I'm going back to my modest job as mayor," SpongeBob announced, dropping the spatula on the floor. "New Kelp City needs me."

"Mr. Krabs," cried Squidward with delight. "I brought back the number-one fry cook. You've got to pay up!"

"All right. A deal is a deal," said Mr. Krabs grumpily, handing the golden egg over to Squidward.